Nursery Rhymes
Yankee Doodle
and Other Best-loved Rhymes

alphabet soup

an imprint of

WINDMILL
BOOKS

New York

Published in 2009 by Windmill Books, LLC
303 Park Avenue South, Suite # 1280, New York, NY 10010-3657

Illustrations by Ulkutay & Co. Ltd.
Editor: Rebecca Gerlings
Compiler: Paige Weber

Publisher Cataloging Data

Yankee Doodle and other best-loved rhymes / edited by Rebecca Gerlings.
p.   cm. – (Nursery rhymes)
Contents: This little piggy—Yankee Doodle—Higgledy, piggledy—
Twinkle, twinkle, little star—Three blind mice—One for sorrow—Little Tom Tucker—
There was a crooked man—Rock-a-bye, baby—Three young rats—Georgie Porgie.
ISBN 978-1-60754-122-6 (library binding)
ISBN 978-1-60754-123-3 (paperback)
ISBN 978-1-60754-124-0 (6-pack)
1. Nursery rhymes 2. Children's poetry [1. Nursery rhymes]
I. Gerlings, Rebecca   II. Mother Goose   III. Series
                398.8—dc22

Printed in the United States

For more great fiction and nonfiction, go to windmillbks.com.

CONTENTS

This Little Piggy

This little piggy went to market.
This little piggy stayed at home.
This little piggy had roast beef.
This little piggy had none.
This little piggy cried, "Wee, wee, wee!"
All the way home.

Yankee Doodle

Yankee Doodle went to town,
Riding on a pony.
He stuck a feather in his hat
And called it macaroni.

Yankee Doodle, keep it up,
Yankee Doodle Dandy,
Mind the music and the step
And with the girls be handy.

Father and I went down to camp
Along with Captain Gooding,
And there we saw the men and boys,
As thick as hasty pudding.

7

There was Captain Washington,
Upon a slapping stallion,
Giving orders to his men,
I guess there were a million.

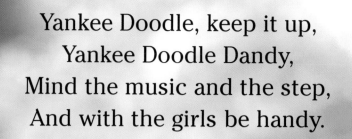

Yankee Doodle, keep it up,
Yankee Doodle Dandy,
Mind the music and the step,
And with the girls be handy.

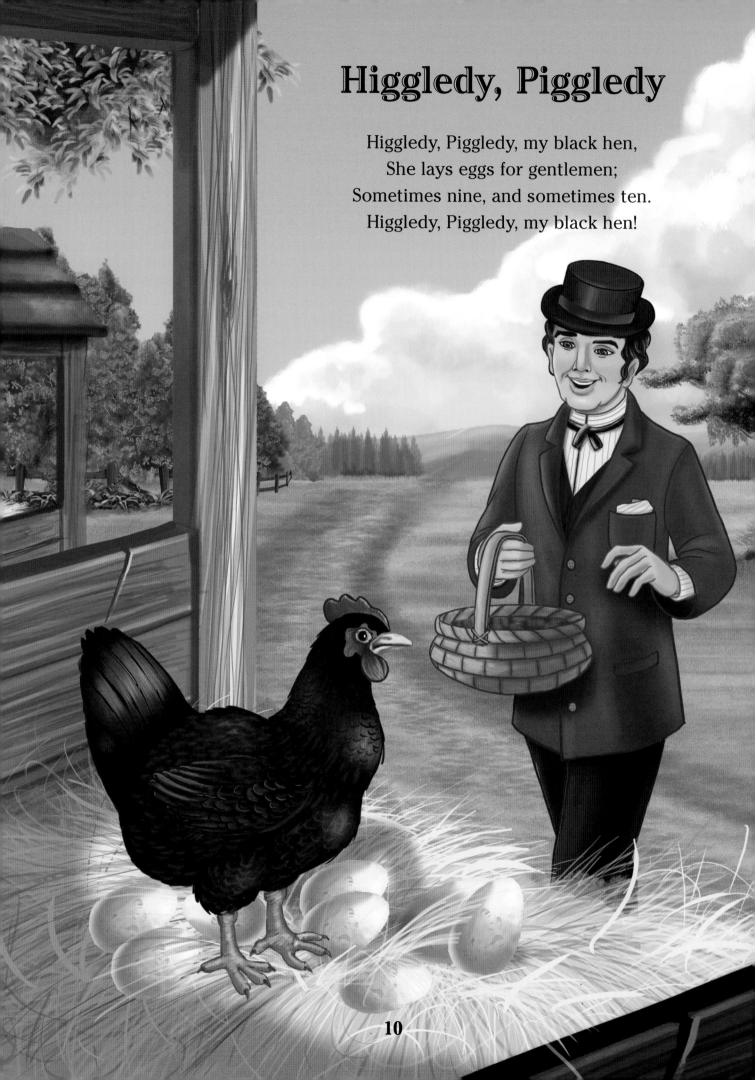

Higgledy, Piggledy

Higgledy, Piggledy, my black hen,
She lays eggs for gentlemen;
Sometimes nine, and sometimes ten.
Higgledy, Piggledy, my black hen!

Twinkle, Twinkle, Little Star

Twinkle, twinkle, little star,
How I wonder what you are.
Up above the world so high,
Like a diamond in the sky.
Twinkle, twinkle, little star,
How I wonder what you are.

When the blazing sun is gone,
When he nothing shines upon,
Then you show your little light,
Twinkle, twinkle, through the night.
Twinkle, twinkle, little star,
How I wonder what you are.

Then the traveler in the dark,
Thanks you for your tiny spark.
He could not see which way to go,
If you did not twinkle so.
Twinkle, twinkle, little star,
How I wonder what you are.

Three Blind Mice

Three blind mice, three blind mice,
See how they run, see how they run!
They all ran after the farmer's wife,
Who cut off their tails with a carving knife.
Did you ever see such a sight in your life,
As three blind mice?

14

One For Sorrow

One for sorrow,
Two for joy,
Three for a girl,
Four for a boy,
Five for silver,
Six for gold,
Seven for secret,
Never to be told.

Little Tom Tucker

Little Tom Tucker
Sings for his supper.
What shall he eat?
White bread and butter.

How will he cut it,
Without any knife?
How will he marry,
Without any wife?

There Was a Crooked Man

There was a crooked man,
And he went a crooked mile.
He found a crooked sixpence
Against a crooked stile.

He bought a crooked cat,
Which caught a crooked mouse,
And they all lived together,
In a crooked little house.

Rock-a-Bye, Baby

Rock-a-bye, baby,
In the tree top.
When the wind blows,
The cradle will rock.

When the bough breaks,
The cradle will fall.
Then down will come baby,
Cradle and all.

Three Young Rats

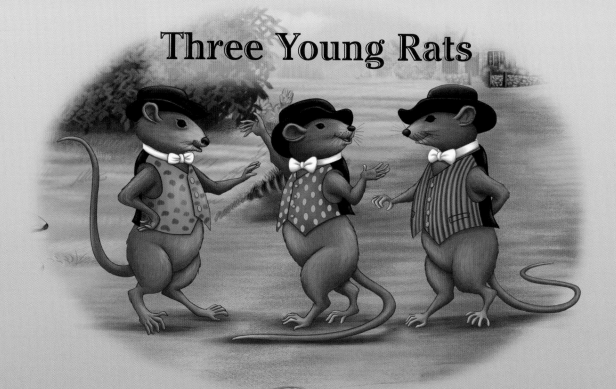

Three young rats
With black felt hats,

Three young ducks
With new straw flats,

Three young dogs
With curling tails,

Three young cats
With demi veils,

Went out to walk
With two young pigs,

In satin vests
And sorrel wigs.

24

But suddenly
It chanced to rain,

And so they all
Went home again.

25

Georgie Porgie

Georgie Porgie, pudding and pie,
Kissed the girls and made them cry.
When all the boys came out to play,
Georgie Porgie ran away.

ABOUT THE RHYMES

Children have been reciting nursery rhymes for hundreds of years. These rhymes have been shared across generations, and they are an integral part of most people's childhoods. Surprisingly, nursery rhymes are often more than just playful verses. In fact, many nursery rhymes in this book originated with historical events.

Nursery rhymes were often used to make fun of political events during times when more direct challenges of authority carried serious consequences. But the social and political criticism was so subtle that most people thought the poems were nothing more than simple children's songs. As a result, nursery rhymes form an enduring link between the present and the past.

Because the rhymes were passed down orally, there are many different interpretations of their meanings. The following are the most popular interpretations of some of the rhymes in this book. If you're curious about the other rhymes, see what you can find! Each rhyme tells a unique story.

Yankee Doodle

The origins of this rhyme date back to fifteenth-century Holland and a harvesting song that began, *Yanker dudel doodle down*. Later, the song poked fun at English Civil War leader Oliver Cromwell. The word *Yankee* was a mispronunciation of the Dutch word for *English*, and *doodle* refers to a simpleton. But it was a British surgeon, Richard Schuckburgh, who wrote the words we know today, ridiculing the colonists fighting in the French and Indian War. Soon after, the British troops used the song to make fun of the American colonists during the American Revolutionary War (1775–83), but the colonists adopted it as a rallying anthem of defiance and liberty.

Twinkle, Twinkle, Little Star

First published in 1806, "Twinkle, Twinkle, Little Star" was written by two English literary sisters, Ann and Jane Taylor. Together, the pair wrote many nursery rhymes in the early 1800s, and this touching nursery rhyme has become one of the most well-known and well-loved of them all. Since it was penned, it has become a popular children's song with a simple, easily recognizable tune. The phrase "like a diamond in the sky" creates a vivid picture of a shining, jewel-like star and is regarded as a great example for young people of how words can fuel our imagination.

Three Blind Mice

The three mice at the center of this tale were in fact three Protestant noblemen found guilty of plotting against the English queen, Mary I. The queen was given the nickname "the farmer's wife" in this rhyme due to the large estates she owned. She was a devout Catholic who had a fearful reputation because she persecuted those of the Protestant faith. She was also referred to by the less than flattering title of "Bloody Mary." Although the rhyme suggests that the three Protestants were blinded and their bodies dismembered, in reality they were burned to death at the stake.

There Was a Crooked Man

The references in "There Was a Crooked Man" date back to the reign of the English Stuarts and the life and times of the English king, Charles I. The crooked man is believed to be Sir Alexander Leslie, who was a Scottish general during these times, when there was considerable ill feeling between the English and Scottish people. Leslie signed a covenant that ensured Scotland had free reign over its religious and political affairs. The stile that is mentioned is said to represent the English-Scottish border. The rhyme ends with a state of peace having been reached and both sides living together side-by-side in a "little crooked house."

Rock-a-Bye, Baby

One interpretation of this rhyme is that it reflects the observations of a young pilgrim boy who had seen Native American mothers suspend birch-bark cradles from the branches of trees. By hanging the cradles in the trees, the mothers allowed the wind to rock their babies gently to sleep. Another suggestion is that the rhyme dates back to eighteenth-century England and refers to a family who lived in a hollowed-out yew tree called the Betty Kenny Tree in Shining Cliff Woods, Derbyshire. The parents, Kate and Luke Kennyon, had eight children and are reputed to have hollowed out a bough of the tree to act as a cradle for their many offspring.